My Heart's On Lock

By: Soulja Choc & Chey

ISBN-13: 978-1979364270

ISBN-10: 1979364273

LIL' RICCY

I walked out my cell mad as a muthafucka thinking about that bitch. I hated my baby mama, Kayla with a passion; she was just so fucking childish. If it wasn't for my daughter, I would have been had the bitch killed. It was like her sole purpose on this earth was to drive me crazy. We had a one-night stand, and that was all it was supposed to have been, but this bitch put a hole in the condom. The crazy thing was, I didn't even know she was pregnant. I found out about my daughter, Terrion when she showed up to my mama's house, talkin' 'bout she needed money for our baby. Psst... I waved her off and told the bitch to bounce with that bullshit. I hadn't seen her in over a year, and here she was with this supposed six-month-old baby.

"Kayla, I'm not 'bout to argue with you. You wanna come around after all this time talkin' 'bout some baby. That shit don't even seem real. Get the fuck outta here. You were a one-night stand....shit, gone wrong."

"Gone wrong? Nigga, you trippin'. See, I knew you was on some fuck shit, but you had a little bit of money, so yeah, a bitch was trynna Rake It Up! I poked a hole in the condom, so now, yo' ass is stuck with me. Shit, we can get a DNA test, 'cuz baby, Terrion is 100 percent yours, nigga!"

We were yelling so loud, my mama heard us arguing and came out the room to see what was going on. She walked up behind me and heard what I had said to Kayla. She took one look at Terrion and slapped the shit out of me. She pushed me out the way and invited them in the house. I was so hot, I just stormed out the house. I went to my nigga's house and

2

grabbed one of my guns and went searching for an enemy. It took me two hours to catch a nigga slippin'. I was ducked down on the side of a dumpster, patiently waiting for him to come out the store. He came out talking to some slim bitch like he wasn't in a war zone; that nigga was playing.

As soon as the girl walked off, he walked towards his car without a care in the world like he forgot how real shit got around here. I waited until he got in his car, and by the time he put his keys in the ignition, he saw me running up and he reached for his gun, but he was a little too late. My gun was already aimed at his head. As I pulled the trigger, he tried to duck down. I got him once in the head, then ran up to the car and hit him two more times for good measures. I knew that nigga was dead, so I ran off. I was laying low, waiting for them to talk about him dying on the news, but Allah must have been with that fool that day because he survived. The streets were talkin'; I knew the bitch had seen my face. I wasn't goin' take no chances on her snitching on me. I started secretly hunting her day and night, that bitch was hard to find. Three months later, I finally caught the bitch walking out of Walmart. This bitch was right under my nose the whole time, working five minutes from where I was hiding out at. I watched this bitch for a week, then I found out she lived alone, and I had to catch her going straight home from work. I was goin' make sure nobody saw me this time. I had fake plates on my rental car and a ski mask In case I had to jump out or do some cream shit. I knew about another week of following her, I would have her figured out.

I wasn't worried about the nigga; he was a gangsta, so I knew he wasn't doing no snitchin'. He killed one of his homies for being a snitch. Every time I would get close to thinking I had this bitch figured out, her routine would change up. I had something for that bitch though. I baked this bitch a cake. I went and got at one of the smooth as pretty boy homies and had him get at her. In no time, he was taking her out to eat, to the movies, and all that good shit. I came out my pocket with a rack, I wanted to make sure he wined and dined that bitch. I needed to beat her at her game; it was like somebody told her I was hunting her down. It took two weeks for him to get her to give him some pussy, now I was goin' be able to put my plan in motion. I was goin' have to move fast, didn't need this nigga catchin' feelings. The bitch was bad, I can't lie, with a monster ass. I had this nigga go to her house to pick her up one night, and he left the back door unlocked for me, then left and took her to the movies.

3

When they left, I waited about an hour and a half and hopped her back gate, went to the door and twisted the door knob. Like he said, it was open, and I went in and waited.

Around midnight, he pulled up playing his music loud like he wanted people to come say something. He waited till he got there to tell her he wasn't comin' in. She was mad, but she tried to play it off. He waited till he saw someone look out the window, then he gave her a passionate kiss. She got out the car, he got out with her, and walked her to the front door with his music blasting. At the door, he gave her one last kiss. As he walked to his car, an old lady yelled, "If you don't cut that music down, I'm goin' call the police."

"That's what's wrong with old people these days, all always talkin' 'bout callin' the police. Bitch, call the police then," he said as he laughed getting in his car.

"You goin' to hell," the old lady yelled back.

I was in her room behind her door, waiting for her to come in the bedroom. It seemed like she was taking forever. She used the bathroom and some more shit, each second seemed like a minute. I was like... this bitch needs to hurry up. About 10 minutes later, she finally came waking in, and I didn't waste no time. I came from behind the door and put the bitch in a choke hold and lifted her off the ground. She tried to yell, but the grip I had around her neck wouldn't allow a sound to come out. She tried clawing at my arm; good thing I had on a long sleeve sweater. Her body went limp, and I held her another two minutes before letting her go. Once I let her go and her body hit the floor hard with a thud, she didn't move at all. I knew she was gone, but I still felt her wrist for a pulse. Now that I knew she was dead, I exited the house the same way I came in and disappeared. Now that she was gone, I could go back to my normal life. I finally could breathe again. Now it was time for me to have my baby mama bring my sons to see me at my mama's house.

The homie I had set the bitch up, my little nigga caught a dope case a week later. I went to visit him, put money on his books, and all. I asked him if he wanted me to bail him out or get a lawyer, and he chose to get bailed out. I was a real nigga, so I bailed him out the same day. He got out but was scared to hustle since he had a case pending. That nigga was seriously goin' let a public defender represent him. That nigga was crazy. I gave him my opinion and let him do him. I did my part for my young nigga. If he wasn't willing to take a chance to make the money to help him, how could I give him my money I made doing what he didn't want to do to get it? I had my sons to take care of. That nigga ended up getting lucky, they threw his case out, and I was happy for him, until they came and raided my mama's house and took me to jail for murder and attempted murder. It was because of niggas like him that I didn't really fuck with niggas no more. Had me doin' all this time, and after all these years, I was finally goin' get to spend Christmas with all three of my kids together.

Loon looked at me and said, "Where yo' mind at, big homie?"

"Trippin' off my daughter's mama, Kayla. Man, if it wasn't for my daughter, I would have that bitch killed before I get out," I said with a cold look on my face.

"It's really that bad?"

I rubbed my hand across my face and said, "My nigga, you don't know the half. She's the reason I'm in prison." Kayla constantly had me checking niggas about her whorish ways, loving the crew and trying to fight my girl. Kayla never knew how to act like a lady; that was one of the reasons I didn't date black girls now.

"I thought it was behind Frog. Why you have me paralyze him then?" he asked with a frown on his face. "That was my best friend's big homie".

"No, 'cuz didn't snitch, I tried to kill Killa Moe because my mama slapped me hard as fuck because of that bitch, Kayla. I was mad and went on one. I just wanted to take my anger out on somebody."

"Damn, that's crazy, big homie."

"After all that, this bitch still put me through all this drama, this bitch made me leave my son's mama, Stacy, just to be a part of my daughter's life. I didn't want to, but I had to. My baby mama Stacy told me she understood, but after a while, she started trippin'. I played along until my daughter turned four and knew who I was, then I told her mama to suck my dick."

"Damn, that's deep. I told you to get on Tagged and get you a white girl or a Mexican."

"Ya'll niggas be killing me with this white girl and Mexican shit. I can see a Mexican bitch, but a white girl, my nigga?"

"I love white girls, them the best ones. They listen and don't put you through all the drama. Shit, if you had a white girl as a baby mama, she would bring your kid' up here together and make sure yo' kids know and love each other."

"Nigga, you crazy, lil' nigga."

"Just give Tagged a try; I bet you knock a bad Mexican or white bitch."

"I might just do that."

JESS

"*G*ood morning love, I have laid out your attire for the day, and your coffee is beside you. Don't forget, we have dinner plans this evening with my boss and his wife."

With my eyes closed, I rolled them thinking, Oh, joy, joy. Just how I envisioned spending my night, seeing as I was young, childless, and should be living life. I was tired of everything that Freddy and I did had to do with his boss, even vacations. I always thought that meant time away from the people at work, well, for normal folks, but you see, Freddy was everything but normal.

I had met Freddy when I got off probation a few years back. I was living life somewhat recklessly and some of what I had done caught up to me. Thankfully, they was minor things. He was running a program for females with a record and assisting them with finding a job and bettering life. Not wanting to deal with someone clocking my moves daily, I had signed up and figured I would give up the street life and turn over a new leaf. Don't get me wrong, I love that part of my present life. What I didn't like was the boredom that came with it.

One night after a seminar that was held with different companies that was willing to hire individuals with records, I stayed back to help clean up. Some of the attendees had left a big ole mess behind. No class or respect, I tell ya'. How hard was it to take your trash with you or place it in the garbage can?

"You really don't have to do that, Jess. I'm used to this; this is my fifth seminar since I took the job as an assistant to Councilman Jones. I want to better our community, and I wish many of the clients in this program we run would see they are worth something; they just need to accept change."

"Well, I appreciate it. I think what you are doing is great. And honestly, I don't mind helping pick up. It's not like I have anything better to do at the moment. My friends are all busy this weekend."

"Well, if you want, maybe we can grab a coffee and something to eat when we finish. My treat, of course, and a way to thank you for helping," he offered.

I really didn't want to go home and become a couch potato, so I figured why not? It couldn't hurt, right. He wasn't bad on the eyes. He was respectful and cared about the community. I wanted to try dating again, and date someone different from what I normally looked for. I had a thing for thugs. Something about a man in jeans, hoodie, and some Tims who didn't give a fuck turned me on, but that also came with broken hearts, lies, trouble, and baby mama drama. Why not try the suit and tie kind of guy?

I actually had a great time, and the conversation flowed. He was very respectful and attentive. His manors were on point. He opened doors, pulled out my chair, and he even suggested a few drinks and some of the entrees they offered for me to try. Had I known this would become my life, literally, I would have run the fuck away. He would suggest things to limit my choices. In a way, it was a control thing without being cruel with it.

He was a lover without a doubt. He waited until we got married for us to consummate our union. He was always tender when we made love. Notice how I said made love. For the most part, it was missionary position. He would gaze into my eyes, and he had even cried. He would take his time, and something told me if he went hard core, he wouldn't last for more than five minutes. I tried to take control one night, and he got mad and went and slept in the other room, said he felt like less of a man. So, to avoid an argument, I would go along with it, pretend I was satisfied, then when he would knock out, I'd creep out the room, find my stash of toys, and bring myself to climax.

Freddy wanted us to start a family right away; he was trying, but I made sure I took care of that. I was taking birth control. I wasn't ready. I wanted to live life. Travel and have fun, which brought me back to the start of this chapter. Here I was climbing out the bed, looking at the plain outfit he picked out, knowing it would work for cocktails later with the lame crew. His boss was older than my parents, and I'd much rather hang out with them. I got that he wanted to one day become a councilman himself, but I was just not satisfied with what came with it.

I lost so many friends when I got with him and later committed to Freddy. He didn't like my choice in people. They were all trouble and ruined the world. He could say that about some of them, but not all. I did have a few friends that lived life without breaking the law, but he even found things wrong with them or the person they dated. Don't get me wrong, Freddy was a great man; he really was. I was given everything and anything I wanted. He would bathe me, shave me, wash my hair, and paint my toes. He would cook, clean, and do laundry. If only he would loosen up some, then it would be great.

While sitting outside at the little eatery we were at, located in Back Bay Boston, I saw my friend Trinity walk by. Glancing in all the nearby shops, approaching us, she asked me if I had seen her husband inside, which I had not, and told her such. She told me she would call me to fill me in on what was going on. She turned around and down the street she went.

"Well, that was mighty rude of that woman," Clarence said.

"I agree, she clearly saw us sitting here enjoying a couple's dinner. Maybe she should be with her husband instead of looking like a mad woman searching for him," his snotty wife co-signed.

"Actually, she is an amazing woman. Very well respected and comes from a good family," I had to put my two cents into the conversation with the judgmental people of the table I was at.

"Well, I must admit this was a great evening, but I have a long day tomorrow looking over different locations for the new youth center that is due to open up soon, so we need to bow out earlier than usual," Freddy stated.

I was happy as hell to be able to get the hell out of that place. The music was tasteless. I wanted to go home and strip and relax, and have something stronger to drink and hit up my girl and really see what was going on. I honestly never saw her looking the way she did tonight.

Once we got home, Freddy went in on my ass bitching about how embarrassed he was, and I needed to put my people in check. I just waved him off, went and showered, and climbed in bed with my phone to find out the details. Apparently, she had been seeing signs of her husband having an affair and asked me if I would help her. I told her we had to meet up for lunch this week and hung up. Freddy came into the room, showered, and once in the bed, he turned his back to me and went to sleep. Thank you, Lord, because I really didn't want to be bothered with him the rest of the night.

LIL' RICCY

*L*oon and I ran laps around the track. We were tryin' to stay physically fit. I was going home in less than a year, and Loon only had a year and a half left. Niggas didn't understand why Loon and I were as close as we were because of the age gap and because I just met Loon when he came to the prison where I was. What they didn't understand was this may be the first time meeting him in person, but I had spoken to him years back over the phone. When I had to explain to him that his best friend was a snitch and he took it upon himself to handle his best friend rather someone else handle him. Ever since that day he handled his best friend who was now in a wheel chair, Loon came to prison behind it. That was why I had been going out my way to see to it he was straight.

Now, back to this workout. After we had ran seven laps around the track, we stopped for five minutes to catch our breath. Then, we walked over to the bars. I jumped up first and pulled myself up and did it 15 times which sounded like nothing, but the average dude struggled to do it five times. After Loon got down from doing his 15 pull ups, we walked over to the dip bar, and I jumped on that and did 25 dips. When I got down, Loon did the same thing. We then went over to the push up bars, doing a set of 25 pushups, and as you already know, Loon followed suit. We did our rounds of each set of bars 10 times.

We finished our workout, we walked to the fountain, and washed our hands and drank some water, and went and called next on the handball court. It was one team ahead of us. We patiently waited for out turn. When it was our turn to get on the court, the new dude on the yard wanted to bet $50 on a game. I wasn't all that good at handball, but Loon was a beast, so I raised the bet to $100 because where I was slacking, I knew Loon would pick up. We got on the court, we scored the first point, and they quickly flew by us, and the next thing we knew they had us 5-1. It was looking like they were 'bout to win my hundred dollars. I was thinking I was going to lose the money, and just when I was ready to just give them the game and go play some basketball, Loon began to work his magic. He scored two points and made it 5-3. They in turn scored again bringing it to 6-3. Next thing you knew, it was 11-7, and the game only went to 15 points, and we won that money. They scored two more points bringing it to a close game 11-9. We scored another one. They did another one bringing it now 12-11. Then Loon scored three points straight ending the game.

The dude who lost the money looked at me and said, "You a bum," basically talkin' about how I couldn't play well, then he turned towards Loon and said, "But you, you're a beast."

Loon was cocky about his game, and before he could respond, I spoke up saying, "I may be a bum, but I'll be a bum spending that hundred dollars."

He smiled and said, "You paid; get it like Tyson."

He must have thought because I was twice his age that I was going to let him get at me like I was a busta, so before he could even blink his eye, I charged at him. His partner knew who I was, so he jumped in the middle of it to stop it and said, "Don't trip, homie. You goin' get your money."

By this time, my homies and his took notice and rushed towards the handball court. When they got over there and found out what happened, me and my homies were close with his, so instead of us all getting into it over his homies, we decided to DP the homie, so two of them rushed him, and we backed up until the police came over. They were still going to make him pay the hundred dollars. The police had us all on the ground until they had us under control. Once the incident was under control and escorted the three inmates to the program office, they resumed yard. Everybody went back to what they were doing before it all went down. About 10 minutes after that, they announced yard recall, and we all walked back towards our buildings.

I walked in the building with Loon and another homie. Once we got inside, telling them I'd catch them later, I headed to my cell. I grabbed my shower shit off the door and went to take a shower. I took me a quick shower and went back to my cell, put some lotion and deodorant on. Then, I threw my thermals on. I went to my stash spot, pulled out my phone, and turned it on. I called my mom and kids to check on them. Then, I said fuck it, let me give this Tagged shit a try, and made me an account. I set me a profile and began to view the profiles. I left a couple white girls and Mexican girls some messages. Then, I logged out and figured I would check back later on tonight or in the morning to see if any responded.

JESS

I had plans to meet up with Angel after work to see what was going on with her and her husband. I had never met him in person. You see, Angel and I knew each other since middle school. We always remained in touch. I had only seen her husband via social media. They got married around the same time as Freddy and I, and since Freddy didn't like my friends, or me being around them, not even for special occasions, I wasn't able to make it to the wedding.

We were at Dunkin Donuts having a coffee and she was telling me how he began to keep long hours at work, phone was always locked, and paycheck didn't add up to extended hours. She wasn't sure what to do. She just found out she was pregnant, and before she told him about the baby, she wanted to know if he was indeed having an affair. I felt bad for her; I truly did. I told her I had wished I could somehow help her, and she smiled big.

I knew that look. It was the look that had me grounded a few times growing up. She was scheming. She had some crazy plan in her head she claimed was safe for me and would help her. She wanted me to make a few social media pages and send a request to her husband and see if he would flirt back or even worse, try to meet up, and if so, she was going to be the one to show up. I told her I would, but I couldn't use my married name.

She snapped a few photos of me and we went to work setting up the pages. On one particular site called Tagged, I was getting messages back to back. I ignored them, but once we found her husband, we began to flirt with him. He was active, so it didn't take long for him to send a message back. At first, he wasn't really saying anything horrible. Just basic

14

things, his age and what he did for work. He asked how was my day and a few things about me.

My phone alerted me of a text message, and it was Freddy, letting me know he was getting worried. It was late, and he wondered what time was I planning on coming home. I assured him I was on my way and told Angel I would keep her posted. Then, once Freddy went to bed, I would really see if I could break her husband down. We said our goodbyes, and I went home.

The night was no different than any other one. Dinner, the news, and a boring session of love making. He went to bed, and I crept out the bed, grabbing my phone this time, and headed into the living room. I logged back into the website and saw I had a ton of messages. One caught my eye; it was from a very attractive older man. Something about his picture grabbed my attention, so I clicked on it just out of curiosity. I learned his name was Lil' Riccy. He was actually incarcerated. He was hoping that didn't deter me from writing back. He added he was due to be released before Christmas, which was in about eight months. I just wrote back a simple hello and clicked out and went in search of Angel's husband so I could see if he was really meeting women off the internet.

Little did I know then that this was a life changing day for me. A day that so many things in my life would flip upside down, but I wasn't complaining.

LIL' RICCY

I laid on my bunk in my prison cell thinking about the women I had been through since I'd been locked up. Some, we just grew apart, and some I pushed away because of their lies. I was a realist, so I didn't care if my girl went and got her a little dick here and there. I wasn't giving her permission, but I also wasn't trippin'. If the shoes were on the other foot, I'd make sure I visited, send packages, and make sure she had money on her books, but I'd also be giving this dick a party. I'm just keeping it real, something most niggas wouldn't do. These niggas around here be demanding things from their girl, knowing their girls don't have it or can't get it at that moment. Those are the niggas I don't respect; got their women runnin' around trying to get money for their lazy ass man.

What dudes don't understand is, that the women are doin' this time with us. I actually believe it's harder on them than it is on us. They're the ones spending countless nights crying to their friends about missing us or being lonely. Sometimes, they just want to be held. Visits helps out a lot, but what about when we're in the hole or on lockdown, when we can't get visits, or can only get behind the glass visits? That shit ain't really nothin' to me, but it kills the women. I've hurt some women, I've also been fucked over by a woman. I watched my women closely, but I didn't lose trust in women for what other women have done. I give women a chance to show me if she's worthy of my love or a piece of my heart.

I enjoyed reading, writing, listening to music, working out, playing sports, and getting my mind mentally ready for the Free world. I saw so many dudes go home and come right back to this hell hole. It was a lot of us that would love to have the chance to do a couple years and go home. I've been locked up over 10 years already, and mostly everybody else has been locked up just as long or longer than me. It was dudes in here that were innocent and would never get a chance at going home to their family that would love a chance at freedom. I stopped talking to some of the short-timers; I got tired of hearing all the "Bro, I am not never coming back," then I look up six months to a year later and see the same stupid muthafucka walking in the yard.

That was why I didn't deal with most of these niggas. I mostly stayed to myself and dealt with the handful of real dudes I fucked with. All these dudes wanted to do was talk about what they had on the streets, how many bitches they were fucking, and how many dudes they shot or killed. I really lived that life; I didn't want to hear about that bullshit. Talk to me about some money or how we goin' get out of prison? That was the type of shit I wanted to talk about. These dudes wanted to run around here trying to impress each other. While they were running around here wasting time, I was chasing that bag and my freedom.

In my free time, I made lighters out of pencil and wire, draw cards, and make window blockers, then I'd sell them to the niggas around here. That was how I got made a living for myself in here. I sent my drawings to the streets to be sold, and that was how I took care my kids from behind these walls. I was close with my whole family and real close to my kids, especially my daughter. If I went a week without talking to her, she wrote me going off in a respectful way. She didn't understand that these phones were illegal, and we weren't supposed to have them. The only time she didn't trip was when I was in the hole, and that was because I wrote her a couple times a week. All three of my kids stayed in contact with me, no matter what their mothers were talkin' about.

Now, I got a lot of women mad at me right now. I fell back and wasn't trippin' on women, something that shocked everybody that knew me. Especially since I'd been a playa my whole life. I just got tired of the games and drama. My mama, cousins, and a couple of my homies would visit when I wanted a visit. Shit, some of them just popped up. A couple of my homies in here told me I needed to get me a Mexican or white girl, I would always laugh at them. Then I let them talk me into jumpin' on a dating site. That was where I met Jess, a white girl from the hood. She'd been holding a nigga down with no drama. I should've dated outside my race a long time ago.

She was different than all the women I'd been with. She was smart and very family oriented like myself. She loved writing, so I got plenty of mail, and sometimes I got a couple of letters in the same day. I didn't even have to ask her. With black women, you had to beg or threaten them to write. Their favorite excuse was "You always callin', baby," then when I say, "Well, I ain't goin' call," then I'll get a couple letters, and it'd stopped again. If I told her to handle some business, all I had to do was tell her was once, and it was done. She'd really been on her shit, and don't get it twisted, she wasn't no punk bitch. If I raised my voice too loud or tried to check her, she would get right back loud with me and check me back, and I respected that. She earned it.

JESS

I was really tired of living this way. I was no longer happy in my marriage. I felt like I was drowning each and every day. It was also not fair to keep holding Freddy back from finding someone who could give him what he kept asking me for. I often wondered if it would be possible to love again. Would I ever meet someone who would come into my life and with the blink of an eye change my whole outlook on things? Knock all these layers down? Huff and puff and knock down the brick wall that I had built around my heart?

Those were questions that I had asked myself that led me to meeting Lil' Riccy. It was about six months ago when I had joined Tagged trying to help my friend catch her man cheating. I uploaded a few simple pictures of myself and filled out some basic questions about me, you know, the simple stuff like what I love to do and so forth. I never imagined I would begin to talk and interact with some of the men, but I did. I guess I was seeking something I felt Freddy was lacking. The drive to achieve something in life, ambition, to be great, and succeed.

Well, this was how I met Lil' Riccy. In a matter of a week, I had put Freddy out of my home, and in a month's time, Lil' Riccy was constantly on my mind. We would spend hours sending messages back and forth, even pictures. He would make me laugh and just feel free. I loved how he took life for what it was. He didn't take anything for granted. He lived for the day and appreciated just waking up seeing the next one. He was bright and had dreams that he was aiming to achieve.

Lil' Riccy was black, but that wasn't out of the ordinary for me. I was attracted to color. He had a smile that would light up the darkest of nights. He had a pretty boy, yet thug look to him. He wore his hair in shoulder length dreads. He had some suckable lips and deep dimples. He wasn't tall, but that was fine because he was taller than my 5'2". He had a huge personality. I was falling and falling fast. I was afraid. I walked down a similar path in my past, and I was hurt like no other heartache before, so I was trying to fight what I knew I couldn't with Lil' Riccy. He was irresistible, and wouldn't accept me quitting what was brewing. It was either I was all in, or he was walking. I chose to ride, and I had no regrets.

This had been the happiest I had been in forever. Lil' Riccy was like a blessing, but one thing stood in the way of us. Not distance, not me being married, not even us being different races. He was in prison serving a long sentence. Many had called me a fool, even Freddy. They asked why was I willin g to devote my life to someone I had no guarantee to have a real future with outside of the walls? Simple, because in my heart, it felt right, and he made me happy. That was all that mattered. He was real, raw, and he was true. That was all he could be.

It'd been six months since we met. We went from just messages and exchanging pictures to actual phone conversations. That, in time, turned into phone sex, and then actual video sex. He made my body feel things many lovers in my past were unable to achieve, and all Lil' Riccy used were words. He was able to stimulate my mind along with my body. I couldn't wait to be granted permission to go and visit him in person because I knew if the chemistry was this electrifying over electronic devices, then once we connected in person, it would be hard to contain us. I envisioned so many things I wanted to do to him, and I could feel my clitoris jump with each and every thought.

It felt like I belonged right there. He was the missing piece to my puzzle that would complete me. I just needed to figure out how this was going to work. I knew it would be a long, rough road. Being with a man who was incarcerated wasn't easy. But from that first visit, I knew even more, and with no doubt, I was going to be his rider, and my heart was on lock.

LIL' RICCY

*T*he more I tried to walk away from this crippin', the more I got pulled back in. It was a solid young Crip up here named Loon, he got the heart of a lion, but the younger homies around his age thought he was soft because he wasn't into fighting homies. They would clown and try to make fun of him, but that didn't bother me, but the little homie Chip called Loon a bitch today, and Loon was so mad that he started crying. That made all the other young homies start laughing at him. I could tell he wanted to fight badly, I knew what he needed. I usually didn't get in the youngstas' business, but I couldn't help it this time. I walked up to Loon and said, "Nigga, you either goin' run that fade, or you can't stay on this yard."

Loon got up, wiped the tears away, and walked off. The youngstas started laughing out loud, thinking he was about to go roll his property up and tell the guards he couldn't be there. He went to the cut where niggas went to fight and called Chip. All the young homies turned around looking shocked; he was doing something they were all scared to do. Chip was bigger than Loon, he headed towards Loon knowing he was about to smash him. Loon just stood there waiting. Chip stopped, pulled his gloves out his pants, put them on, and took a few more steps to get to Loon. Loon wasted no time; he threw his hands up in a fighting position, and Chip did the same as they squared off.

Chip rushed in and caught Loon on the side of the head, and Loon back peddled but stayed on his feet. Chip rushed him again and pinned him on the wall. Loon with his back against the wall couldn't do anything but swing back, but he only threw a punch here and there. Chip was punching the shit out of Loon. Loon was blocking most of the punches, but some connected. Loon's nose started bleeding, and once he tasted blood, it was like he turned into a different person. He threw a few wild and crazy punches, and one of them hit Chip in his big lips. Loon split his upper lip open like a hot link that got boiled too long. Chip wasn't used to getting hit hard. He took a step back, Loon grabbed him, and spun him around to the wall. It was Loon's turn now.

Loon was skinnier and faster than Chip. He went to work on Chip. Chip tried to block the punches, but Loon was too fast for him. After Loon had his mouth and nose busted, I grabbed him off of Chip. Loon was pumped up now, and he wanted some more, so he called out another one of the homies who always picked on him. Ears and Loon were about the same size, but you could tell Ears was scared. He was bully number two, but seeing what just happened scared him. Loon didn't wait, he just rushed Ears. Ears backed up, but he was throwing punches back. He caught Loon on the chin with a good one, and Loon went down. He jumped up so quick you would think the ground was on fire. They fought for another minute, then we broke it up when they got to wrestling, but they wouldn't be messing with Loon anymore.

The guards let us fight as long as we went to the cut where the Sgt, Lt, or Captain couldn't see. After that was over, dinner was comin' up, so we needed to get ourselves ready for that. The other homies around my age washed their hands with the little homies. I just let them just do their own thang. I wasn't bangin' like that anymore, but I wasn't goin' let them make the hood look bad. I was from ASD, Asian Street Dragon. We were mostly Asian, but about 25 percent of us were black. We all took our Crippin' serious though.

I had a job; I was a yard crew worker, meaning I got showers after work. The people that didn't have jobs had to bird bath after yard. That was washing up in the sink in their cell. After I got out the shower, I put some lotion on, then laid in my bed for 10 minutes to relax. After that, I got up and grabbed my phone out my stash spot and cut it on. I waited so all my messages and inboxes from messenger to pop up, then I responded to all of them including one of my stalker ex- girlfriends. Then I laid back and called Jess, like always, she was happy to hear from me. We told each other about the day's events, then we started talking nasty to each other. She loved when I talked nasty to her, especially when I called her my bitch. She always said that got her pussy wet.

I had only sent her pics of my dick, which she knew it as Monster. She was a freak, and she always wanted to see Monster. I was a freak too, so I wasn't trippin'. I was in the cell by myself, so I told her to get naked and call me on Tango, she said, "Okay Daddy," and hung up. I stripped down to my boxers, and the only other thing I left on were my socks and shoes. I put my window blockers in the window so nobody could see in my cell if they walked by. I didn't have to worry about the guards; whenever they came in the tier, it was a call we made to let everybody know they were on the tier. Everybody did all kinds of illegal shit, so we all looked out for each other whether we fucked with each other or not; we all hated the law.

She called me on Tango. She was used to me watching her play with that pussy, so she was on her back with her legs wide open. I watched her with my phone in my left hand, and as I watched her, I grabbed Monster out my boxer hole and stroked it with my right hand. I licked my tongue at her and said, "Beat that shit up for me."

She smiled and said, "Anything for you, daddy," as she started sticking her black dildo in and out of her pussy faster.

"Is you my bitch?"

"You know I'm yo' bitch. Stop playin', you know I'm whatever you want me to be."

"What's my name, bitch?"

"Daddy...Ooh Daddy, I'm cummin'."

I let her get hers, then she was getting ready to put it in her ass when I switched cameras. She saw Monster and jumped up and put her face all in the phone. She looked at it with wide, open eyes, and asked, "Are you trying to give me a heart attack?"

"Bitch, shut up, and put this dick in yo' ass."

"You know I love when you talk to me like that." She laid on her back, leaned up, and looked at me as she eased her dildo in her ass. She stroked it nice and slow until she saw me starting to go faster. She was tryin' to match my stroke. "Damn, this shit feel good, Daddy. I'm about to cum again."

I waited till she came again, then I told her she could watch me now. She put the phone up close to her face and watched as I did my thang. I started going faster. I could feel it rising through my dick like lava coming up through a volcano. It was coming. "Yeah bitch, I'm 'bout to cum." I started killing myself.

"Yeah, put it all in my face, Daddy."

"Open yo' mouth, bitch. Here it comes." I came, and cum shot everywhere.

JESS

I felt someone climbing in my bed. I could smell Lil' Riccy, so there was no need to panic.

I just rolled over onto my side from my stomach. I always slept with no panties on, and he knew that. It was good to let the pussy breathe. Anyway, back to what I was saying, I got on my side because I knew to assume that position. Daddy loved that when he came home from a long day of being out on the block making it do what it do. Stacking that paper so we could continue to live the lifestyle we were.

"Good girl, I see you listening to Daddy," Lil' Riccy said.

Wack! He smacked my ass, but it didn't bother me. He loved to see the ass cheeks jingle, and if it made him happy, I was happy.

Now he was right behind me with Monster as we called that third leg of his, right at the entrance of my naturally wet entrance. BAM! Not taking it slow or easy, he rammed into me causing me to lose my breath, but I quickly gained it back. He was pounding me from the side, holding my left leg up just a tad bit so he had more access to go deeper and faster. I began to throw it back at him matching him pound for pound. Daddy loved the fact that I wasn't a coward or scared of the dick, and I always put work in right with him.

"That's right, bitch, I can see you creaming on my dick, but I want you to let it all out. Stop fucking playing with me, Jess before you piss me off. You don't want me to get mad, do you?"

"No Daddy, don't take my dick away. I promise I'm close to cummin'. Keep fucking me harder! Deeper!"

"You better, bitch, because I want to see you get five of them off tonight, and if you punk out, that's going to be five weeks of no treats."

He did that often. He would pick a number of times he would want me to cum, and if I couldn't hang, which I will add was very rare, he would punish me for the same amount of weeks he wanted me to cum. I guess tonight was five. To date, that had only happened twice, and I was off that Henny dick, and hours had passed, and I honestly couldn't take any more. My man was a killer in the streets and definitely in the sheets.

"Right there, baby. Go...fucking...harder!" I screamed as Lil' Riccy was hittin' my spot, and I was losing it. I was stuck, not able to even move anymore for the moment. I just wanted to savor the feeling of his perfect 9-inch-thick dick hit where it was repetitively, and moments later, I came, and I came hard.

"Aight bitch, that is one down. Now come taste your pussy juice," Lil' Riccy said as he laid onto his back, and I crawled so I was between his legs.

I looked up so I was staring into his face. He loved that eye contact shit, but more so, when he was in control and fucking me. He loved to see when he hit it and got those omg faces from me. I started from the base of it and licked from there all the way to the tip, then popped the head in my mouth and right back out.

"Don't play games, Jess. You better suck this dick."

"You told me to taste it, didn't you? I'm savoring it," I replied.

He grabbed my long hair and pulled me up so I was looking him right in the face.

"Get smart again, Jessica."

"Boy stop, and let me go. I got my nut, don't you want yours? You know that talk and pulling hair just turns me on more, that shit don't scare me."

He just laughed because he knew I was right and let me go back to handling business.

Once I was back down where I was and comfortable, I wasted no time, seeing as he didn't want special attention, and I began deep throating him while grabbing his balls and massaging them. Letting them go, I moved my hands to create a circle around his shaft and had my mouth just covering his head and sucked gently while using my hands in a circular motion, going up and down stroking him.

"That's right, just like that. This is what Daddy wanted. Just what I need."

Three minutes later, he busted all down my throat. I swallowed every last drop and came up licking my lips asking, "What do you want next, baby?"

"Climb on top, and don't you stop, bitch, till we both cum. You hear me? I know this going to be a challenge because your ass cums real fast when you ridin' me, but you need to learn control."

Placing both feet flat on the bed, straddling him, I eased down and began to bounce slowly. He did say I couldn't stop until we both came, and I wasn't trying to bring on an early climax, so I was planning on going slow. Well, of course, when it came to Lil' Riccy and sex, nothing went according to my plans.

"Bitch, what the fuck is you doing? You ain't new to this shit.

You better ride this shit." As he grabbed my hips tighter forcing me to bounce faster.

Being that I always aimed to please him, I rode and rode him as if I were trying to win a derby. Once we both came in that position, which I did get two off on, he flipped me so I was on my knees. This was where I was going to be in trouble at. He gave zero fucks in this position.

With my stomach flat on the bed and my arms reaching outwards, ass tooted in the air with my legs spread, Lil' Riccy smacked both ass cheeks yet again and then began by going in deep, then coming all the way out to do it all over again. He did this about a dozen times until I begged him to just go on and fuck me and to please stop teasing. But naturally, he had to dominate in the bed, so he just grabbed his dick and used his head and was moving it up and down my pussy, from my clit to my hole stopping right there acting like he was going to enter only to move back up. The last time he did that, I moved my ass back and gripped his dick hard with and began to fuck him. I didn't know what he thought, but he wasn't going to play with my pussy like he didn't want me to play with his dick.

"Oh, it's like that, Jess, huh? You just goin' take your shit. Go on then, mama. Do your thing," he said.

"Baby, please fuck me back. I want to really feel you, even this is a tease," I whined but still continued to back it up on his dick.

Granting me what I was asked for, Lil' Riccy went to work on my pussy for another 35 minutes--even after I came another three times and felt like my legs were going to cave. Just as he busted all up in me and fell on to my body, I heard a phone ringing.

"Hello baby, good morning. How did you sleep last night?" Lil' Riccy asked.

"Ugh baby, sleep was great. My dream you just woke me up from was even better. So good, I need to shower and wash the sheets," I replied

"Crazy girl, what you talkin' about now?"

"Baby, it felt so real. You were here, and we were fucking for hours like animals. It's like I can still feel you inside me. I can't wait until they release you so all these dreams can become a reality."

"Me too, baby. Me too, but I have to get up off the phone. I just wanted to hear your voice this morning and send you off to start your day right. I'll talk to you later, Jess. Be good, and keep my pussy on lock."

"All of me is on lock, and you already know it. If you need me, send me a message. Bye." With that, we hung up.

These dreams I tell you be so real. I had to get up so I could take care of what I needed to do because if not, I would've lay in bed all day thinking about the warm, nasty dick that should've been inside of me.

LIL' RICCY

I woke up at five a.m., and the first thing I did was get out the bed and stretch. I put me on some hot water then washed my face and brushed my teeth. I took me a gangsta, and for those that don't know what that is, I took me a mean ass shit. I got done handling my business and washed my hands up, and made sure they were clean; that was a must. I got me my cup and put two spoons of Folgers coffee inside and added the hot water. I wasn't the average prisoner; I didn't drink it black. I drank a Cadillac, I added some cocoa and sugar and added a Three Musketeer candy bar. I took a sip of my coffee and got the boost that I was jonesing for.

I took my shirt and sweat pants off and put on some gym shorts and began to jog in place. This CO lady came by to do her six o'clock count, but she stopped at my door and was staring hard inside the cell. I looked behind me as I continued to jog in place to see what she could have been looking at but seen nothing out of place. I looked back at her and threw my hand up like what's up, she glanced down at me and walked off. So, I looked down where she looked down and laughed because I caught on to what had her stuck. She was watching my monster bounce all around in my shorts as I was jumping. She wanted it. Once my adrenaline was pumping, I started to do burpees which consisted of 100 pushups broken down to two sets of 50. Then 100 jumping jacks, 25 back arms, then 25 squats. I repeated this until I had 1000 pushups done.

I put my window blockers up and got naked and took me a quick bird bath. Five minutes later, they opened up my cell door for breakfast. I had walked out my cell and met up with a few of the homies and walked to the chow hall to eat breakfast together. On the walk over, we joked and laughed, you know what I'm sayin'? We sat at the table and ate that bullshit ass breakfast they tried to feed us. Well, some of us did. Others like myself had brought some cereal with us and gave our trays to those that couldn't afford to get canteen.

After we were done eating, we just were sitting at the table talking and bullshitting for about five more minutes, and that was when I noticed the homie Chip whispering to the others sitting with him at his table. I was trying to figure out what he was talking about, but yet, not trippin'. I put it off until I saw him in the yard later on in the day, but I was going to see about it because I wasn't feeling the way some of them were looking our way.

Making our way out the chow hall, we got to the building and dapped each other up and went our separate ways until later. I walked in my cell and cut my TV on and took my prisoner shirt off and left on my sling shot. I turned my cd player on and put in some R. Kelly. I put the volume where only I could hear it loud and it be clear. I then walked to the door, looked out the window, and watched everyone run around until they were locked up. Once they were locked up and the coast was clear, I went to the stash spot and grabbed my phone. The first person I always called every morning was my kids. I wanted to make sure I spoke to them before they left out for school and wished them a good day. Next call was to my mom's. After that call was complete, I called Jess to holla at her while she got ready to go into work; another every day normal routine in the morning. She had my dick up telling me about the dream she had last night.

We laughed and joked during the time it took her to get ready and leave out for her job. She sat in her car outside and kicked it with me seeing she had some time to spare before she had to go in and clock in. I liked that about us. Conversations could be serious, sexual, or just funny. She definitely had a sense of humor and was always joking around.

Once we hung up, I went to YouTube to check out the homie Menace's new video. I put my phone up afterwards. I was proud of him; he was doing it. I had to get ready for yard time in 15 minutes. We went to yard, and I met up with the homies at the normal spot we usually gathered at. I got up and went by the court to watch a game of a few people play basketball, and I happened to look over, and I saw Chip whispering yet again and stealing glances my way, and I began to wonder what their issue was because they now had my attention, and I knew I had to address the situation and see just what the problem was.

Putting two and two together, the only thing I could think it had to do with was the fight he had with Loon. I was watching these two little niggas, but they weren't watching the lil' homie Loon that won the fight, so by them not watching them, I was now seeing they were going to try and pull some sneaky shit.

I walked to the spot I had in the yard where I stashed shit, and I poured some water on it to loosen the dirt so I could grab my shank and went back to watch them at the court. When the homie Chip was walking off with the group he was with, I saw them laugh and head toward the young homie Loon, so I headed that way too. I approached Chip, and now we were arguing back and forth, and I couldn't believe he had the nerve to act like he didn't know any better.

Chip said, "You actin' like you takin' sides, Lil' Riccy, when we grew up on the same block."

"Yeah, you the homie, but right is right, and I'm goin' always keep it a buck," I spat back.

"You on some straight bullshit, Lil' Riccy. Real talk, dawg," Chip responded.

"If I'm on some real bullshit, I'd be stabbing niggas for getting at me like this, and niggas already know it."

"Is that a threat, Lil' Riccy?"

Looking at Chip, I replied, "As you just stated yourself, you been knowin' me since you was just a little nigga playing on the block, so you already know the answer to that question. I don't make threats, nigga. My word is my bond. I make promises."

They took a step towards me, and I pulled out my knife, and as soon as that happened, it stopped what they had planned which was a three on one match with me. I gave him that look that said Go on and move, and I'm goin' light your ass up.

JESS

*W*alking into work with a smile spread clear across my face, my girl, Marissa, whose desk was next to mine, looked up giving me that *Okay girl, spill the tea* look.

"Let me guess, Jess, you just hung up with Lil' Riccy?" she asked me.

"As I do every morning," I sang, then added, "Am I that transparent, though?"

"Since you have met him, yes. You been glowin', but I love it, so no complaints this way because it makes it that much easier to work with your ass. I don't miss the old married Jess who was a miserable, married bitch that carried negative energy in these doors every day."

"Well, that's no longer going to ever be the case," I replied as I was logging into the system and began to process the paperwork that was left on my desk by my supervisor and answering to emails.

Seeing Marissa still looking at me out the corner of her eyes with a smirk on her face, I took out my compact mirror from my purse looking over my face trying to see if I had something on it. Not seeing anything, I looked at her and said, "What? Nothing is on my face, my shirt is buttoned right, and my shoes are matching...what is amusing to you?"

"I am still waiting on the tea, Jess. Yes, you have that I am lusting over my man look, but today, it's more than that. Something new happened overnight, so spill it," she said.

"You sure you work in the right field? I think you need to be reading tarot cards or looking into crystal balls or something. If it will get you to stop staring, I'll tell you, gosh. I had my first wet dream last night. I swear it was so real. Amazing actually, and I swear if Lil' Riccy is half as good as he was in the dream, then I am in trouble when he comes home."

"Get the fuck out of here, Jess. That good, huh? Well, I am happy for you. If anyone deserves to be happy after all the shit that's happened, it's you, girl."

"Thanks, girl. So, what's new with you? Still screwing the boss behind his wife's back?" I asked laughing but low.

"Yes, and I'm getting tired of it to be frank. He wants me all to himself while he has his fulltime family he parades in my face. I can't do this much longer."

"I say leave him. Find someone for you. You're beautiful, Marissa."

"And what, lose my job? I can't do that. Who will pay my bills, and I have 2 kids to feed. I can't take that loss even if it means sacrificing true love and happiness."

I felt bad for my girl. She got the job because she had met our boss, Chuck at her old job. She was an exotic dancer. She was new to the state and got a job at the club until she could find something more promising. Chuck met her on her second week and gave her a position here. Now, it'd been two years, and every time she talked about leaving him, he told her she could go back to shaking her ass. He told her he would see to it she didn't get another job in the area, and he had the pull to do such. She was a single mother raising a son and daughter. The kids' father was gunned down during a drug deal gone bad, and she took off for the safety of her kids.

"We goin' figure something out, Marissa.   If I have learned anything these past few months it's that in life, we have to take risks to find happiness." She just nodded and got to work, and I did the same.

****

Walking in the door, I placed the keys and my purse at the table by my door and hung up my jacket and placed my shoes in the jacket. I proceeded to my bedroom to put on something more comfortable to get ready to prepare a small meal for dinner. I was making chicken Alfredo and broccoli. As I was heading back toward the kitchen, I heard my cell ring and the caller tune indicated it was Lil' Riccy, and not wanting to miss the call, I picked up my pace and made it just in time.

"Your dime, my time," I said into the receiver. "What you say?" he asked.

I repeated it, and he laughed, and said, "You crazy, but what you doin'? How was work today?"

Running down the events and a brief version of me and Marissa's talk, he told me wasn't too much I could do to help her but be her friend. When she was really tired of it and made the steps to leave, then she would, and I would be able to offer more help. I had to agree with him. See, this was another quality I loved about him. He always gave me sound advice, and it made sense. Telling him I was about to start dinner, he told me he was going to call me on Tango so we could cook together. I hung up and waited for the app to notify me he was calling. I got out the ingredients, and as I filled the pot with water to steam the broccoli, I was connecting our video.

"I can't wait until you are really here, and I can feed you, baby," I told him "Not as much as I can't wait to be able to be there and actually eat that and more, if you know what I mean, girl."

"You crazy. You goin' have to eat food, Lil' Riccy, to have the energy to do all what you be sayin' you goin' be doin'."

"Oh, I'm goin' eat, but it will be your juices that gives me that burst I'll need. But let's get back to cooking before you burn the house down."

Approximately 45 minutes later, I made myself a small portion and put the rest up for lunch the next day. I put the pots in the sink to soak while I ate and made my way into the living room.

"That plate has my stomach growling, baby. Let me make me a soup real quick; don't start without me," Lil' Riccy said. "Okay, baby."

Once he was back in view of the camera, I asked what movie to put on, and he said Belly. He loved this movie. We ate our food, and I positioned my phone on a stand where he could see me and the TV. Finishing my food, I placed my plate on the table and tucked my legs under me and laid back grabbing the phone with me. Half way into the movie, I must have fallen asleep because I was woken up by Lil' Riccy calling my name telling me to go on into the room and get some sleep.

Before doing such, I washed the dishes and hopped in a quick shower and climbed in the bed, all with him still on the phone and laid down. I wasn't sure when he hung up because again, I fell asleep, but I know he waited until I was good and knocked out because in the morning, I had a text message about how he loved to watch me sleep and see my chest rise and fall in between each breath. It was the small things that made me love him, and I wished I could see myself the way he saw me.

LIL' RICCY

*A*fter I hung up with Jess, I sent her a quick text so she would see it in the morning and put my phone in the stash spot. I had a lot on my mind. I knew shit was about to go down in the yard the next day, and being as I only had one tool, I needed another one, so I got up and prepared to get ready. I got some weapon stock which was a little piece of metal that I had broken off a fence. I straightened it out and once I did that, I sharpened it to the point that even the tip would prick your finger if you touched it. I added a handle onto it, and then put them both side by side. One was designed like an ice pick, and one was flat like an actual knife. The ice pick was great because when you stabbed a fool, it would be hard to detect and could lead them to bleed internally. I was getting ready for war. I was a one-man army when I needed to be. They didn't call me a soulja for nothin'. I then rolled my mat out to get ready to call it a night. I wanted to get enough sleep where I could be extra aware of my surroundings the next day. I stripped down to my boxers and socks, brushed my teeth and put my durag on and hopped up on my bed setting my two shanks at the end of the bed.

****

I woke up with the same shit on my mind and did my every day morning routine. In the chow hall for breakfast, I had a light weight stare down with them little homies, but it wasn't nothin'. I was with my homies, so it would be fair. They were just a table away from ours, so if they really wanted to jump, they could. Chip smiled my way like he was saying it was all good, my nigga, I'm a see you in the yard later, and I nodded, then said out loud, "Why wait? I'm ready now." Then smiled back letting him know I was 'bout whatever he was, and all he had to do was say or make a move, and it would be on like popcorn. He shook his head no, and said, "Nah, we goin' wait till yard."

I went back to my cell after breakfast and got my phone to call my kids. Then I had called my moms and Jess to let them know a situation was brewing with me and a little bitch ass nigga in his feelings, and if shit went bad today in the yard for them to be sure to look out by sending me some stamps, paper, and envelopes because I'd be in the hole.

They both tried to plead with me to just chill and brush it off. To walk away from it, but I had to do what I had to as a man. There was no way I was going to let anyone play me like a sucker or speak to me like I was some pussy bitch. Once I broke it down that way, them both understood and assured me that they had me no matter what. I could hear the extra concern in Jess's voice. This was the first time she had heard or seen me like this. My moms, however, knew how I was. It was kill or get killed in my mind.

I tied me a holster on both my legs next to my balls and put my knives in place. I walked to the yard ready for whatever. We were goin' see if he really wanted this smoke with me or if he was just talking like many had in the past. I met up with the little homie Loon and one of the G's I rocked hard with, and we walked towards the rest of the homies to get shit poppin'. When we got close, I put both my hands in my shorts ready to whip out my knives. Seeing my movement, this big ole dumb nigga goin' say, "Let me holla at you alone for a minute, Lil' Riccy."

We walked over to the side while all the homies stayed and watched. I still had my hands in position in my pants, but this time, my hands were on my knives, and I was ready to pull them out on this fool. He began to talk to me, but I wasn't really payin' attention to what he was spitting. I was watching his movements more. He was keeping his eyes on my waist at the same time because he knew what it was. He knew like everyone else knew I didn't play. Chopping it up for a few minutes, him basically pleading his case, and me just nodding my head because I really didn't feel like spending time in the hole, we agreed to let it go. He didn't want the smoke; I knew he was just putting on a show. I was still goin' keep an eye out though because wasn't nobody 'bout to catch me slipping or sleeping. I stayed woke. The rest of the yard time went by smooth, but my eyes were trained and stayed on the movements of Chip and his homies. I needed to keep up with their whereabouts.

When yard was over, me and the homies all gave each other dap like always and went our separate ways. That was one thing I couldn't stand about this prison shit; niggas be so quick to get into it with a homie, but when shit got too real for their ass, they wanted to work shit out. I could only imagine what bullshit he fed his bitch crew for them to not look at him sideways because if someone in our crew did some bullshit like he did, we would definitely side eye his gangsta.

  I promise I couldn't wait to be set free. I was tired of dealing with part time fake ass gangstas. These young ones got dumber and dumber and made us older ones look foolish right along with him. They were beginning to make us all look bad.

JESS

Getting that phone call from Lil' Riccy this morning about what was brewing up there had been heavy on my mind. I wasn't getting any progress done at work. I was worried sick. Was he in trouble? Would this lead to him having to serve more time if he killed someone? My greatest of all the possible fears was if he was hurt? I wasn't sure I could handle that kind of news. I just found my knight; I couldn't lose him already.

"Hello Jess, are you here, or did you get lost? You have been staring at that cell phone and barely doing any work since you got here. What's up? You definitely aren't the new and improved Jess I was just talking to yesterday before walking out the doors, so can you kindly return her?" Marissa had said as she passed by my desk but not before placing a fresh cup of coffee on it.

"Thank you, girl. I just have some things on my mind, and I can't focus. But sitting here not getting work done won't fix what's on my mind. I have zero control over it. I can only pray on it."

"I'm sure whatever it is will be okay, girl. Now, get to work because Joe's father is coming in the office today, and I'd hate to see you get in trouble for not meeting the quota."

"Thank you for the heads up. I'm going to go run to the ladies' room and sneak a quick call. Cover for me, okay?" I said as I stood up while putting my cell phone in my pocket and headed to the bathroom. I wanted to check in with Lil' Riccy's mother to see if she had heard from him. Maybe he hadn't checked back in with me because he knew I was at work.

"Hey baby, what's going on?" his mother, Anna asked, answering the phone. She was such a nice, sweet lady. Although we never met face to face, we had many conversations over the past few months.

"I was hoping you heard from your son. I'm sneaking this call in while at work. I can't focus and was just told the big man will be in the building, and I can't afford to fool around and get fired for not working, but I'm stressing."

"If I know anything, honey, I know that my son is just fine. That boy was born with survival skills. He is going to be just fine. I wish he didn't make many of the choices he did in life, but you go on and do your work. I'll text your phone if I hear from him, but don't you worry about him," she told me.

Not feeling that much better but knowing it was all out of my hands, I thanked her and headed back to my desk. I took a sip of my coffee, sat my phone face up so I could see any notifications received, and just went to work. I was already two hours behind when I sat back at the desk, but before lunch, I had caught up and was actually ahead of my workload.

I stayed at my desk during my lunch break and browsed the internet. I didn't have the taste to eat anything. Marissa rolled her chair over to me and basically told me to just let it go. Whatever was weighing heavy on my mind, just release it. I just looked and said, "It's Lil' Riccy. I'm scared. He called and told me he had a little problem with some guy and I'm afraid I'm going to lose him. I can't lose him already, Marisaa."

Unsure of where they came from and not even knowing they were on the bridge of dropping, I felt two lone tears fall from my eyes. Reaching for a tissue, she handed it to me and told me there was no way he was going to leave me already and to think positive. Lil' Riccy wouldn't want me this upset, and she was right. I knew I needed to be his strength, and I shouldn't be showing any signs of weakness. If I couldn't have faith and believe in him, then what did that say about our bond? I wiped those tears real fast and smiled a real genuine smile and thanked her.

The rest of the day of work flew by, and before I knew it, I was walking out with a raise and feeling great. The only thing I needed was my phone to ring and to hear his voice. I rushed home through rush hour traffic. I brought my phone with me into the bathroom getting ready to my nightly shower before preparing a small meal. I placed my phone on the window seal that was next to the shower just in case Lil' Riccy called, and I climbed in.

While washing my hair, my phone rang, and a rush of relief took over my body as I heard the song "Crush" by Usher and Luna play. I had programmed that as Lil' Riccy's caller tune when we first exchanged phone numbers. Snatching the phone up, I quickly answered it.

"Baby, oh my god, baby, I been goin' insane. What happened, are you okay?"

"Calm down, mama. Do you know who your man is? I'm good; that boy aint want no real smoke with me. Nothing happened, but I came back into my cell after yard time and knocked out. My mama just told me you called her from work. Girl, you know you're crazy, right?"

"Crazy for you," I replied.

"What you doin' right now, Jess?" he asked.

"I'm actually standing in the shower. I didn't want to miss your call, so the phone was close by."

"Is that right? Well look, I want you to put a leg up on the side of the tub and do what Daddy loves for you to do. Take two fingers and insert them in you."

Doing as I was told, I gasped as my fingers entered me. He heard it and said, "That feels good, don't it? Well I want you to keep going and don't stop until I say you can, you understand me."

Nodding my head as if he could see me, I kept finger fucking myself, and it was feeling so good.

"You didn't answer me, bitch! I want you to keep going until I tell you to stop, and daddy is right here stroking monster, so I'm right with you," he said with more base in his voice.

"Yes daddy, I won't stop until you tell me to."

"That's what's up, baby girl. Now, make me proud, and let me hear how good it feels."

I knew what that meant. He wanted me to bang it, so I began to go hard. The sound of my juices and the water from the shower mixed was loud, but my moans were louder.

"Are you close to cummin' Jess?" Lil' Riccy asked.

It was as if he could see me because I really was. "Yes baby, can I cum?"

"Yes, you may go on and let it go. I'm cummin' with you."

Once I released, I washed up with him on the phone. Turning the water off, I got out and wrapped a towel around myself and walked into the bedroom.

"Baby, you scared me today. I was so afraid I was going to lose you."

"I'm not going anywhere. You got me, Jess." Nothing else really mattered after those words. All the stress and worries from the day was washed away in the shower and wiped out my mind with that "You got me, Jess remark.

LIL' RICCY

I was lying on my bed looking at the wall thinking about all the shit that had been going

on around me. I knew the homie Chip really wanted to get the young homie Loon because he did beat his ass, but they now knew in order to get to him, they had to get me too. Where they were into fighting, they knew I had no problem with ending shit quick and stabbing, and they really didn't want to lose their life or cross the line. I hated having to think like that, but it was the life I lived. I wasn't the type to sit around and let a nigga try me., I was the type to choose my target and go get it. I always struck before I could be hit.

I didn't want to think about that shit no more. It was stressing me out and one thing I didn't do was stress, so I picked up this urban book called Gutta Squad Lifestyle. It was a part two of a book called Birth of the Gutta Squad by Author Soulja Choc. He was a homie from Watts. I loved his flow with words. He wrote how the life was and gave it to his readers raw and uncut. Just starting part two I was hoping it was as good as the first one. As I was reading, I could see it was definitely a page turner, and I couldn't put it down. They announced it was five minutes till dinner, and I didn't want to pass up no breakfast, lunch, or dinner in the chow hall or even yard time right now with things the way they were. I wasn't goin' give them niggas a chance to get the little homie Loon because I wasn't present.

I met up with my young nigga and gave him dap and embraced him. I was finna hook him up with Jess' daughter. His baby mama ran off on him two years ago, taking his savings and kids. Bitches could be so dirty. When I was describing Mercedes to him, his ears had perked up. You see the difference between me and him was he had dated white girls before and he liked them a whole lot, and he was anxious to get to know her. He didn't have a phone like I did, but he did have some phone time with some people. I lent him my phone telling him I was renting some phone time. I didn't trust everyone or rather anyone to know what I had. If the price was right, anyone was liable to turn on you, and I wasn't trying to lose the $2500 I paid for my shit because of a hater. What money the homie made, he basically sent it off to his mother to help her out and for her to get things for his kids from him.

We went and ate dinner and went separate ways, me telling him he could get at Mercedes when I got my hands on the actual phone. As soon as I was in my cell, I washed my hands and took off my state property shirt. I knew Jess would be up for a while, so I decided to knock out a few more chapters of the book before I called her.

I picked up the book and was reading about when Lil' Seven had got out of the pen and heard about an upcoming homie called DB who was acting like he was running the hood, but he was actually more connected with the other side. They had some words and ended up fighting in the street, but DB had come out on top though. That scene grabbed my attention, so I continued to read more and more, and before I knew it, I had read a couple of chapters, and I knew I had to call Jess before she worried too much and went to bed and trip on me for not calling her sooner.

I would have waited for her to call me, but no matter how many times I told baby girl she could call me, she refused. She said she didn't want to be the reason why I would get caught up with my phone and lose it. This was our main line of communication besides visits, and Jess wasn't tryin' to hear losing it. I put the book down and picked my phone up and dialed her number.

We laid together on the phone for a good two hours until she fell asleep on me again. No sexual shit or anything. That wasn't what we were about only. We just chilled and chopped it up and took the time to get to know one another better and on a deeper level.

Jess told me she needed to holla at me about something important when she came up to the next visit. Naturally, I was curious on what it was about, and I tried to get her to talk about it, but she wouldn't budge. I kept pressing and pressing, but she stuck to her guns and said I would find out when I saw her. She didn't want to talk about it over the phone. Putting some thought into it on my own, trying to take a guess on what it could be but yet knowing it had nothing to do with her being with anyone else because Jess was a rider. She was loyal to the core, even though she was a white girl she from the hood and knew the street life. I knew some of her back ground, and I knew she used to set niggas up to have them robbed and get a cut from it, so nine times out of 10, I was sure that was what she wanted to talk about. I couldn't wait to find out because I was sure either way my girl had a come up for both of us to make some money.

When she fell asleep, I could hear her breathing hard on the phone. I sat on it a little bit longer to make sure she didn't wake up before I hung up. Once I felt it was safe, I hung up, sent my text to her for her to see when she woke up like always, and I stashed my phone. I picked the book back up and didn't go to sleep until I had finished it.   I loved the ending, and I couldn't wait to see what happened next.

The authors writing style was addictive to a homie like myself. He'd be having me picturing myself in the scenes, out in the free world living life like I used to. The only thing I didn't like about these books was the ending and having to wait to see what was next. I was trying to get in his head and think if I had written it what I would write for the next scene, and that was when the idea hit me; I should write books myself. I was definitely going to look into it.

JESS

I swear nothing made my mornings better than waking up to either a good morning baby

text from Lil' Riccy or even a phone call from him. Today, we were having dress down day in the office, which was like a once a month occurrence. I was glad it was today though because I had to bring stuff to the dry cleaners, and I wasn't in the mood for a skirt suit. I sent Lil' Riccy a "Good morning, love" text back and pulled up Pandora and tuned into the Lyfe channel, connected my phone to the Bluetooth speaker I had in the bathroom, and got out my bed.

In the bathroom, I relieved my bladder, grabbed my toothbrush, and entered the shower. I wet my hair and body and then brushed my teeth before I went ahead and washed my hair and then my body. I rinsed off and then rewashed. Pouring a quarter size amount of feminine wash, I cleaned my cookie because I never used fragrance soap in that area, then I grabbed my pumice rock and touched up my feet. I did this every few days even though I always got pedicures done at the nail salon. After finishing all that, I got out and wrapped my towel around my body and grabbed another for my hair, slid my feet into my slippers, and went into the room.

I sat on the edge of my bed and lotioned my body with some Dark Kiss from Bath and Body Works. Well, except for my elbows knees and feet; I used shea butter for that. I also took a little bit of Vitamin E oil and used it on my face. I then walked to my dresser and took out a pair of boyshorts and a bra. Putting those on and grabbing some socks from another drawer, I walked to the closet and took out a floral Adidas sweat suit I had recently purchased with the matching sneakers.

Once dressed, I sat at my vanity and applied just some basic makeup. Eyeliner, mascara, and some lip gloss. I threw some gel into my hair and brushed it into a high ponytail. I was all set for work.

I stood in my floor to ceiling mirror and snapped a few pictures and sent them to Lil' Riccy then I left out the door to head to the office. I knew today would be a hard day for Marissa. Today was definitely a day Chuck flaunted his wife around the office, and today may just be the day Marissa lost it.

I grabbed my lunch from the fridge and an orange from the drawer while I was in there. I guess that would be part of my breakfast. Locking up my door, I was making my way to the car when Lil' Riccy called me, and I answered it. We talked briefly because I was running late, and I needed to focus on the road. Agreeing to talk tonight when I got off work, he wished me a good day and told me I looked nice in my outfit, and we hung up.

Saying as prayer as I walked into the office that I left with my job because I had a feeling today was going to be a shit show, I walked and sat down. I was logged in and already processing payments when Chuck came over to my desk with a pissed off expression plastered on his face. I was unfazed, so I looked back towards my computer and kept working. I helped people rebuild their credit by consolidating all of their bills in arrears into a small monthly amount.

"Have you heard from your little friend Marissa today? Funny she isn't here, phone is going right to voice mail, and she didn't call out," Chuck asked me.

"No, I was wondering why she wasn't at her desk. She normally is here before me every day, but we both know why that is, don't we?" I said to let him know I was very much aware of the situation and the affair they'd been having.

"Look, just mind your business if you want to keep your job. Call your friend and tell her you suggest she gets her ass in here and now, or else her and those kids will be living in a damn shelter because she will be jobless," and he walked away.

I don't understand how the hell she saw anything good in him to even get involved. He was an asshole. I sent her a text, but I got a message right back saying some error shit. Maybe her phone was cut off. So, I picked it up and went against the rules and called her from my desk. Sure enough, it said the number wasn't in service. I hoped she was okay.

Jumping back into work, I figured during lunch I'd just drive to her house real quick and check on her and hope I made it back to the office in time. Although that was the plan, I didn't have to worry about it because I got a text from a random number telling me it was her and she changed her number and would be in the office soon to hand in her keycard. She was quitting. See, I told y'all something was goin' happen today. I felt it.

Right when it was time for lunch, the show started. In walked Marissa with her kids. My girl was not playing. All heads were on her, including Chuck and his plastic wife.

"Can I have everyone's attention please? I am here with my children to make a statement. No matter what I will no longer allow a man to blackmail me into carrying out an affair in order to provide for them. With that said, I QUIT. Go Fuck yourself, Chuck. As a matter fact, please go fuck your wife. I'm fed up with your controlling, over bearing, lame ass. I will go back to the pole if I have to, but at least I will have control over my life."

I started clapping while everyone else was in shock with their mouths open, except for three other females.

"You mean to tell me you were sleeping with her, Chuck?" another girl in the office, Leslie asked. To see the look on his face was priceless.

"It appears my husband here has been doing more than running this company. Let me inform everyone of something real quick. I am the owner; it's my family's company, not his. Marissa, please accept my sincere apologies for whatever my husband has put you through, and I would love it if you would reconsider. You, my darling husband, clear out your office, get the hell out my house, and I'll see you in court. It's over."

Well, this didn't go how I had imagined it would go. Chuck stormed off and his wife sent us all home early with pay. I knew that had to have stung. Marissa and I left out together and took her kids to Chuck E Cheese.

Not keeping track of time because we were having fun with the kids, I was shocked how late it was until I saw Lil' Riccy calling me around the time I was just getting in work. I had filled him in on the day's events, and he laughed. He said he wished he was a fly on the wall to see it. He said I should have recorded it. I told Marissa I was going to head on home because I had a visit the next day with Lil' Riccy and I wanted to get some sleep.

I stayed on the phone with him until I got home. He was telling me how he wanted to look into writing books. I believed in him. I knew that whatever he put him mind into he could do and succeed. He just had that hustler's mentality to him.

LIL' RICCY

I was sleeping so good last night that I woke up late this morning, and since I did, I didn't have time to bird bath before breakfast. Instead of going to breakfast, I decided to stay back and hop in a shower because today was visit day, which began not long after breakfast, and I didn't want to have Jess out in the visiting room waiting on me. When they did call breakfast, I walked out in some shorts and gave the homies dap. I asked my boy to look out for the homie Loon and see to it that Chip didn't fuck with him because I wasn't around. He told me he got it and left out the building to the chow hall, and I headed to the showers.

I got in and took like a 15-minute hot shower and washed out my boxers, socks, and t-shirt. I got out, dried off, and walked back to my cell with just my boxers and shoes on. Once I was in, I hung up my wet clothes on the line I made so they could dry. I put some lotion on my legs, chest, and arms, then put on my clothes for my visit. Once I did all that, I added some Marc Jacob oil so I could go out there smelling good for my girl. I cut some music on low and leaned back and chilled waiting for them to call my name. It took about 30 minutes, and they popped my door open calling my name. I was smiling from ear to ear.

When I got to the visiting room, I gave them my ID and looked around for Jess because I didn't see her. They told me she had gone to the bathroom and to go sit at a table. I went and sat waiting for her to come back, and before she did, I saw a big booty black female walk by me. Her ass was looking so good, I had to take a triple take. As soon as I took my eyes off her ass and looked away, Jess walked up and said, "Hey, baby."

I jumped up thinking maybe she caught me staring at the chick, and I was caught, so I was trying to play it off. I went over to Jess and gave her a big hug and kiss and grabbed her on her ass. After we got done kissing, I pulled out her chair so she could sit down. I then walked around the table and I was waiting for her to give it to me about her seeing me look at big booty girl, and I wasn't as slick as I thought I was, however, she didn't say anything, so I took it upon myself to start the conversation.

Jess got up telling me to follow her to the vending machines to get something to eat. I had grabbed a burger, soda, some chips, and of course a Snickers bar. I loved me some Snickers. She grabbed a bag of chips and juice and said she wasn't really hungry and just wanted to snack on something. We went to the microwave so she could heat up the burger for me. We inmates weren't allowed to do it, only the visitors were allowed to work it. Once we did all that, we walked back to the table hand in hand while I carried the food in my other hand, and she carried out drinks in her other hand.

While I was eating my burger, she was just snacking on her chips and looking at me. She waited until I was finished, and as I was wiping my mouth with a napkin, she asked me if I was ready to talk. I nodded and told her of course I was.

"Jess, I have been wanting to know what you wanted to talk to me about since you first brought it up on the phone the other night, so baby, please tell your man what is on your mind."

Looking me straight in my eyes, which I loved because Jess had some real pretty eyes, she said, "My best friend's husband is up here on another yard."

I looked at her confused and said, "Okay, but what does that got to do with me or us?"

"Well, if you will calm down and let me finish and not cut me off, I could tell you what I was getting at."

"Go ahead," I told her with a slight attitude because I was trying to see where she was going with this.

Rolling her eyes, which showed me she was just as aggravated at this point as I was, she started talking again, "Well, they be gettin' money. I mean, really gettin' money. She just bought a new car. She just closed on a new house. I want to get some money too."

"What do you mean they get money, Jess?" I mean, I had to ask because there were many ways to make money.

"Don't play stupid with me, Lil' Riccy. You aren't dumb by far, so use your head."

"Jess, do you even know what they be doing for sure, or are you just guessing?

"Baby, do you want to make money or not? It's really a yes or no question," she said.

"The question is, are YOU sure YOU ARE ready for this?" I asked.

"Yes. I have been thinking about it for a few weeks, even before I even mentioned it to you on the phone. I wouldn't be bringing it up if I wasn't ready."

"Well then, fuck it; let's do this, baby. Let's get this money together if this is what you want, then I'm down."

"Whew! I was hoping you agreed to it because I have some on me. I already am ready to give it you it."

That blew my damn mind. Who the hell was this girl? I was seeing a whole different side of Jess. I knew she was hood and knew about the streets, but I wasn't expecting all this. I wasn't ready exactly, so I told her we should go buy another burger. I told her to grab the mayonnaise. I popped it open in my hand, and I put it on the bundle she had brought me. I waited until the coast was clear and did my thing. I assured her I had it from this point on, and it would already be handled.

Once I finished my second burger, we went to the podium and asked for a board game. Choosing Dominos, we went back and was playing a few games of it. I let her win so she could think she was doing something. I asked her what exactly she brought me and said I'd find out when I got back to my cell. Returning the Dominos and grabbing some cards, we got in a few games of Blackjack.

Visiting hours were almost over, so we were holding hands and just talking. We both scooted up close to the table and let go of our hands. Jess moved her hand under the table and grabbed ahold of Monster and began to jerk him off with her small delicate hands. It felt so damn good, and it didn't take me long to release in her hand. I didn't see where she put my cum, but now my mind was on feeling on her. My hands unfortunately had to remain on the table. They called visits to be over, so we stood up. I made my way to her, thankfully her hair was to her ass. I wrapped my arms around her lower back and her hair basically hid my hands. I stuck them under the waistband of her pants, and I felt she had no panties on. My girl was a freak. I extended my arm just enough to where I could stick my finger in her ass and before she could holler out too loud, I stuck my tongue in her mouth and muffled the oooohhhh sound she wanted to release.

The police started walking towards us, so I pulled my hands out her pants and rested them on her lower back before we were caught and got in our last goodbye. I told her to make sure she drove home safe, and I would talk to her later. Waving goodbye, she exited the room. I went and took a seat, and when all the visitors left the room and it was just us inmates, the CO's began to call us back in groups of 10. Luckily, I was in the second group to be called. I made sure wasn't no oil residue to be seen from the mayonnaise.

Thinking in my head, Jess was crazy, not only did she bring it up without us agreeing, she did kind of force my hands on it because it was an unwritten rule. Once it was in the room, you didn't send it back out with them. I wasn't mad at her though. She was looking out for us. I was sure she knew I wasn't going to turn it down in the end. That was my girl, and I was proud to say it.

Making it to the yard on the way to my building, I saw the homies, and I walked towards them instead of returning to my cell. I called Chip to the back, and he was mumbling under his breath thinking I didn't catch it. Asking him what was up, he just said it wasn't shit.

Something was off, and I saw that me asking wasn't goin' get me anywhere. I needed to figure out what was going on and soon. I also needed to make the homie Loon some burners. Yard ended not long after I had arrived on it, so I went to my cell, took my visiting clothes off, washed my hands, and waited for them to do count.

JESS

*W*alking to my car, I was happy. I knew Lil' Riccy was shocked and wasn't expecting that. He more than likely thought I was going to talk about some stick up shit, but that was behind me. This was a whole new era, and really he couldn't do too much behind the wall himself to help me if that was the route I was going. You couldn't trust everyone, and that was a dangerous game, so if it wasn't going to be him personally, then I didn't want it to be anyone. Not to mention my boy was murdered behind a lick years ago, and I vowed I would never walk that path again. Those days were behind me the day he took two to the head.

   This thing here Lil' Riccy and I were starting was a risk in its own for both of us. I could get banned and even worse, get arrested, and he could get added time if caught, but I had good vibes we would be okay. We both were very calculated in what we did, which was why I decided to go ahead and just bring it with me before I even got the green light from him. I just felt like I wanted to do more for him than just phone calls, visits, or even phone/video sex. I wanted to see him on top. I wanted him to get his money in more ways than one, to help build his funding even more so he could provide for his children more than he already did.

Pulling off the long path the jail was on and onto the main street leading to the highway, I had to stop at the Concord Jail to pick up my cousin Nikki. I had dropped her and her two kids off on my way to see Lil' Riccy so she could see her kids' father Marcus. He had been incarcerated for a few years, and about a year ago was moved to this facility. With no car, my cousin wasn't able to see him like she was when he was in county, therefore, she and the kids hadn't been by to see him. I ran into her the other day, and I was telling her about Lil' Riccy, and she asked if she could ride up with me, but I dropped them off at Concord and picked them back up afterwards. Naturally, I said yes, so here I was pulling up to pick up her and the kids. She got the kids buckled in and looked at me and took a deep breath. Knowing Nikki, I knew it was going to be something because she always did that when she was trying to control her anger.

"Jess, do you know I have been sitting in that lobby for hours? I couldn't get in to see him because he was already in a visit with some skank ass bitch. I'm going to go off on this piece of shit when he calls me."

"That's crazy. How he have you come all the way up here and have someone else come as well? You did tell him you and the boys were coming today, right?" I asked her.

"No, I wanted to surprise his stupid ass. I guess the surprise is on me. I've been holding shit down for him and our family for three mother fucking years. Since the day his dumb ass got caught, it's been me at every court date. It was me going to county with two kids to see his ass every visit rain, sleet, or snow. This is the thanks I get? Fuck me and his kids for some stripper bitch."

Nikki began to cry, but it was like a... I'm pissed off, hurt and mad ass angry cry all in one. I felt for her. I knew that shit had to be bothering her. She had been busting her ass out in the streets alone. Loyal with kids. My cousin was beautiful, and I was sure men tried on a daily to get at her, and I was sure she shut them all down because she felt like Marcus was just focused on her. He may very well still be. Who was to say this chick wasn't just a pay check to him? Someone to pass his time with and make it easier on Nikki?

"How do you know she's a stripper? Did you meet her and ask?"

I was laughing although nothing was really funny about it.

"Girl, I found out more than her occupation. I got the hoes address, phone number, and place of employment. A little flirting and some cleavage will get you a long way. The CO at the desk gave it up along with his number. Guess he don't like Marcus too much."

"You know what we 'bout to do with that info, Nikki?"

"Sure do. We droppin' the kids off at his mama's house, and I'm waiting for that bitch to get home, and I'm beating her ass. If she thinks she's going to come in and break up my family, she has another thing coming."

"Nah, you ain't thinkin', Nikki. She 'bout to learn that it pays to be with a man with kids. She goin' have to shake that ass a little harder and come up off that paper. Time for you to collect some support for these children. She wants his time, she has to pay his bills."

"Before or after I smack the bitch?" Nikki said.

"Are you paying attention? You are going to kill her with kindness, Nikki. Let me educate you real quick. You will get further feeding her honey than vinegar. You gonna milk that bitch. Feed her thirsty ass the same lies I'm sure he is. He ain't goin' be the only one to profit from the bitch. You sell her pipe dreams greater than the ones he is. Have her eat out the palm of your hands. Have her believe she has a real chance at forever with your man. And when release day comes, you will pull up in the car she helped pay for and ride off with him. He's coming home to you and them boys, and you know it."

"Who are you, and where is my cousin Jess at?" she asked me. "I'm here. I'm back out of retirement. I guess my man is bringing out the logical thinker in me, where I see the bigger picture. You have to think outside the box sometimes and move in a way you wouldn't normally do so to catch them off guard. Find ways to come out on top, cuzzin', in more ways than one. Have more than one plan. So today you will set the plan in motion to become a dairy farmer and milk that cow, and then you're going to crush that dream and let reality hit her hard when she sees you have done nothing but take her ass on a long, expensive ride.

"I love where you are going with this and what you are thinking. This just may work out. Tell Lil' Riccy good looking out because I really wasn't rocking with that stuck up bitch you became. You was lame as fuck. All work and no fun," she said now laughing.

The rest of the ride into the city was chill. We went through a drive thru and grabbed some food for the kids and ourselves and went to Castle Island to sit and eat it. I just watched the planes take off and land at Logan and got lost in thought. I wanted Lil' Riccy and I to take a trip when he got out. I have some planning to do.

LIL' RICCY

I woke up at three a.m. and after brushing my teeth, I washed my face and washed up a little bit. I began to make some burners for Loon. As I was making them, I was wondering why it seemed like the closer I got to getting out, the more bullshit came my way, well not my way, but the people I fucked with. So, in many ways, it was just like fucking with me. I only had a couple of months left until I was free after giving these folks 10 long years of my life. I should be spending this time getting myself mentally prepared for what was to come in the free world, yet here I was awake at this hour making knives like I was just starting my bid not about to wrap it up. After I was finished making them, I spent another 20 minutes putting handles on them, and I tuned into the news to wait until it was time to eat breakfast.

When they popped the doors open, I walked out the cell and met up with my young nigga and passed him the two burners on the low, and we walked to the chow hall together. Once I finished breakfast, I made it back to my unit with no issues which was a good thing. I went into my cell and put on my yard crew vest and went to work. When I got outside on the yard, I was walking around picking up trash until they were about to start releasing the inmates for yard time.

Once inmates began to come outside, I went by my building until I saw my young nigga come out. I met up with him and we waited until I saw the rest of the homies come out to the yard. I pulled two of my OG's from my generation to the side and let them know that I was about to get at Chip and them in a few about the funny shit I still been seeing go on and they showed me they had they shit on them and they was with me.

Myself along with the two OG's and Loon walked over to where the rest of the homies were, and I looked right at Chip.

"Aye, what's the deal, my nigga?"

"Nothing, my big nigga. I'm just out here chillin' getting some fresh air," he responded.

"So, what we gonna do about this situation?" I inquired. "What situation you talkin' about, Lil' Riccy?"

"The situation you think I haven't picked up on where you and your partners feel some kind of way and trying to creep up on the homie Loon and get at him." I let him know I peeped that shit, and I was on to them.

"We ain't trying to do anything to that nigga. You trippin' for real and reading too much into shit that ain't happenin'," he said.

"Come on, lil' nigga, you know I'm way sharper than that, man.

You can't fool me. I know what you plottin' probably before you do." "For real, we ain't trippin' off that nigga and the shit that went down."

"Whether you trippin' on him or not, just leave the shit alone 'cuz I personally like the homie, and I can't and won't let anyone fuck him over like that."

At this point, everyone was tuned into our conversation. Ears took a step towards me like he was taking charge. I didn't think he understood the risk he was bringing to himself by doing such a move. "What you mean, you ain't goin' stand by and let us do anything to him?" he questioned me.

"You heard just what the fuck I said, nigga. Your ears big enough," I clowned him.

"Lil' Riccy, you act like you can't get touched." I guess someone ate their Wheaties at chow today.

Chip turned to his boy and said, "You better watch how you gettin' at my big homie."

59

Ears said, "My bad, my nigga, but he was getting at you kind of foul."

"Nah nigga, he wasn't getting at me foul. He was doing what a real nigga should do when he sees shit ain't right. He was doing what a real nigga supposed to do. You ain't supposed to let your homies jump on your other homies that are young."

Ears took a step back and looked at me. "My bad, big homie. It won't happen again."

Lil' Riccy looked at him and smirked. "It's all good, my nigga. I ain't trippin' off of small shit. It was something I felt needed to be addressed. Now that it's resolved, let's head to the court."

We all walked over to the basketball court. Some were playing a game, others were on the sidelines like myself just kickin' it and bullshittin' watching them run up a five on five full court game placing some bids on it to turn a profit. I made sure to put my money on the youngster and his team, and they didn't let me down. They won three games back to back. He had some game behind him; I'm talking potential NBA type game. Why people even wanted to play against or even bid against him was a dumb move, but a move I wasn't making. The other team ended up quitting, they realized it wasn't a match. We then walked over to watch some of the OG's play hand ball for 15 minutes until they called yard recall. Everyone gave dap and respect and went to their separate buildings.

I walked into mine and grabbed my shower shit off the door and walked to hop into one. By the time I washed up and washed my clothes in the shower, they were getting ready to call count, so they rushed me back to my cell.

I finished getting dressed. I applied lotion and got out a pad of paper and pen and sat down with some headphones on to get started on my hand at writing. I had some shit to tell, and it would make one hell of a good story.

JESS

*I*t was close to Lil' Riccy gettin' released. At times, I felt bad that I entered his life towards the end of his sentence. I wished I had met him and rocked with him the whole 10 years so he could really see that not all females were foul. That may not have been his perspective of me, but then again, how could I be sure that he fully had faith in me and knew that I'd been truthful about everything I said, and all the promises I had made? That was another reason I did what I did when I went to the visit a few days ago. I was big on expressing my thoughts and feelings but also showing them as well. Actions did speak louder than words, and I intended to show him a whole lot.

Leaving work, I asked Marissa if she wanted to come to the mall with me and my cousin Nikki. I wanted to start shopping for Lil' Riccy. He was going to need everything, and I didn't want him to want for shit or have to look for anything. I was going to see to it that my man had it. Telling me that she would follow me that way she could leave right from shopping and go home and not have to have me back track and bring her to get her car, I said ok, but I had to stop and grab Nikki first. She was fine with it, so we got into our cars and headed out.

Arriving at the mall, it was packed. Friday nights were always like this. Everyone was out shopping for outfits for the turn up events of the weekend. Nikki wanted me to go out, but I wasn't in the mood. She had the nerve to tell me I was afraid Lil' Riccy would leave me if I had actually went out to a club, but little did she know, he wasn't like that. As long as I didn't do anything disrespectful towards him and our relationship, he was fine with me living life on the outside. He would actually encourage it.

We were inside Nordstrom, and I was in the men's department getting Lil' Riccy some Balmani jeans and a few pairs of Levi's as well. I also grabbed him some Polo boxers and beaters. I stopped by the cosmetic department and grabbed him some Marc Jacobs and some Joop cologne. Once we left there, we headed to Foot Locker where I grabbed my man three pairs of sneakers and a pair of wheat Timberlands. I stopped off at the Northface store next and grabbed him a fleece and a jacket.

"Damn, Jess. I think I love you. You sure you don't want a girlfriend?" Marissa asked as we were heading into Olive Garden to grab dinner.

"You crazy, girl. I'm all about my man, but why you say that?" I replied.

"Look at all those bags. I know your arms hurt. What damage you do to your account? You definitely dropped a few racks tonight on him." Nikki cut in on the conversation.

"Well, I have it to spend. He deserves it. This is just my way of thanking him for coming into my life and changing it for the better. But can we please order? I'm hungry as hell."

"Yeah, let's eat, but you are going out tonight. I even got Marissa to find a sitter for her kids and agree to come with me. You will never believe what else. She used to work with the girl that was visiting Marcus. This is going to be great. We goin' to the strip club tonight. It's time for me to set the plan in motion, so you know you goin' come over and see this," Nikki said.

She was right; I needed to be there and make sure them hoes in the club didn't try no funny shit when she told this chic she was Marcus' baby mother. Even though the plan was to play it cool, she may be one of those who automatically wants to fight the baby mama. Well, I guess only time would tell. I'd have to let my baby know. I was sure he would be okay with it; after all, it was a female strip club. We finished dinner, and I dropped Nikki off and went home to get ready and wait for my baby to call me so I could let him know about my last minute plans.

Putting the bags with Lil' Riccy's things up in my closet, I undressed and went and got in a quick shower. Once I finished, I sent him a text asking him to call me when he got my message. I walked to my vanity and sat down and began to apply my makeup. I had my hair up in a messy bun not sure how I was going to wear it. I guess I would decide once my makeup was done. Before I was finished applying my eye makeup, Lil' Riccy was calling me on Tango. I answered it, and right away, my baby asked questions.

"Okay, I see you, Jess. Where you gettin' all pretty to go?"

"Out with Nikki and Marissa. They convinced me last minute which is why I wanted you to call me."

"Is that right? You know that you mine, right?"

"Yes baby, and I don't need reminding. I told you already if there is one thing I am, it's is loyal. We were at the mall...I was actually shopping for you, and at dinner, they asked me to go. It's actually a female strip club we're going to."

"I didn't need you to explain anything, I trust you. I was just messing with you. But you be safe, okay? Don't drink too much and drive."

"I don't plan on having anything at all to drink. I'll be driving, and they want to let loose, so they can drink for me. But let me finish getting ready. I just wanted to let you know before I left. I'll text you when I get in tonight."

"Okay, baby."

I finished applying my makeup and decided to put my hair in a high pony. I picked out a red and white one-piece pant set with some red open toe shoes. I painted my toes real quick and tossed my slides on so they could dry. I picked up my shoes and headed out the door. Lord, please let tonight be peaceful and me not have to break up a fight or even worse, have to knock a disrespectful hoe out.

LIL' RICCY

I waited until the coast was clear and went and grabbed the work out the stash spot. I sat it in front of me and shook my head thinking, what the hell did this crazy girl get me into? I began to open the sack to see what exactly she had brought me. I unraveled the tape, and then after that, I undid the fabric softener sheet she had wrapped around the bundle. Then, I unwrapped the saran wrap, and inside of it was seven grams of heroin, seven grams of crystal, and about a half ounce of weed. Jess had made it easy for me by already breaking everything down by the gram, so I decided I wasn't about to do no small deals and waste time sitting on product by nickel and diming it. I was only going to mess with the big boys. She did tell me she already had someone test it, so I didn't have to find anyone to try it for me before I passed it off.

I kept two grams out of the black and crystal and four grams of weed, and I put everything else up because it was nearing the time they would call us for dinner. Once I had that all tucked away, I put the grams I kept out into the little pocket that I had sewn into my boxers, then I went and sat down on my bed and listened to some music until they released us for chow.

When they did open the doors, I went and greeted Loon and the other two homies, and we all walked to the chow hall. While we were in line, I was waiting to see if I could spot my man Pierre, the Haitian dude I used to fuck with to come through. I knew he had money; he was one of the shot callers for the Haitians, and I knew his money was real good. I was talking to the homies, and by the time we got close to the top of the line, I noticed Pierre walk in. I told the homies to go ahead without me, but Loon stayed back. I had to give the lil' homie respect. Ever since everything went down, he had shown his loyalty and respect for me. That's what's up.

Once Pierre was caught up and behind me, I turned in his direction and gave him a head nod as a sign of respect. Something we all did when we held mutual respect for one another.

I spoke first. "What's good, Pierre?'

"Shit, just chillin', been waiting on you to say you back in the game. I miss doing business with you. Not everyone is so clean and easy to work with," he said.

"My man that is just the reason for me waiting for you in line. I got my hands on some shit, and you the first person I wanted to talk business with."

"I like the way you talkin'. What you got, what you got?" he said twice and all excited.

"A couple grams of crystal and some heroin and some bomb ass Kush."

'Okay, I see you, Lil' Riccy. I tell you what, let me get a gram of everything. The money is in my cell and if it's as good as I believe it will be, then I want all of what you got," he stated.

"I have some of it on me right now. Just walk with me and when we reach the bend before turning the corner, I'll pass it, okay?" I instructed.

"No doubt, big dog."

I grabbed a gram of each and handed it off to Pierre. Loon and I then grabbed our trays and went and sat at the table with the rest of the homies. I let them know I had a little something for the same price but not much because some of them had been talking about wanting to get more money. I told them I would need the cash up front though. One of the newer homies was mad, but really, I didn't give a fuck how he felt because I was going to make sure I gave Jess some money, even though she didn't ask for anything in return when she gave it to me. I just wanted to make sure she was good before I made anything for myself from it. Moments later, we were getting up and leaving the chow hall, and as we were walking towards my building, I heard someone calling my name. I stopped and turned around and saw it was Pierre.

"What's up, man?" I asked because I had just made the switch off not long ago and I didn't know what he could need this fast.

He replied, "I did a line of that crystal at chow. I need all the crystal you have, and I will let you know about the black and the weed when I get back to my building and have my testers try it."

Once we reached the building, we stopped and chopped it up for a few minutes longer, and then went our separate ways. I entered my unit and then walked to my cell. I removed my blues and put on my sweats and a t-shirt and pulled out my phone to wait on Pierre to text me with the MoneyPak numbers so I could send the rest of the crystal over to him. I was hoping he would hurry up and hit my line up because it was only an hour and a half before dayroom time, and I wanted to call Jess before it started. I didn't want to miss dayroom; I had a few games of dominos to kick ass in. I sat my phone down, and about five minutes later, I got the text from Pierre asking how many grams exactly did I have so he would know how much to send at once. I told him I had six more of the crystal left so he owed me for seven of the crystal, one of the heroin, and one of the weed. He texted back okay that he was loading the money to the cards and for me to bring the grams to the dayroom when I went. I hit him with a simple aight, and I put my phone up real quick so I could mess with the work.

I never kept my phone out while I had work out. I grabbed the six grams and put the rest of the work up. Grabbing the phone, I saw he had texted me again and said everything had checked out and they loved what he had given them to try, so he wanted everything I had left and what was it. I broke it all down. I told him I had the same amount of heroin as I did of the crystal, but I had 13 grams of the Kush. He said he had half now, and by the time dayroom was over, he could Western Union the rest in whatever name I gave him. I knew I could trust him. He was true to his word and about business like I was. He had long money like I said; wasn't no reason to cheat me out a few stacks. I put the phone up again and went and got all the work this time. I wrapped and secured it together. I pulled my phone out, and Pierre had sent me the numbers to four different MoneyPak's with $500 on each one. He already had confirmation that the other $2200 would be wired when we got back from dayroom tonight.

I immediately called Jess on messenger because while I was conducting business with Pierre, she had also texted me asking if I could call her when I got the chance. I had planned on it anyway; I just wanted to take care of business first. She was getting ready, all glammed up on her way to the club.

"Baby, do you have a Greendot, Rush, or Walmart to Walmart card?" I asked her after I asked her about her plans.

"Yes, I have a Walmart to Walmart, but I haven't used it in a long time."

"Is it still valid? Do you know?"

"I think so, let me check. Hold on, I'll grab my wallet." She put the phone down, and I guess went to get her wallet.

A minute later, she picked the phone back up and confirmed it was still good. I then asked her about a MoneyPak account. She told me she did have one of those because she set one up because the best friend she told me about asked her to, so she could load $500 once for her. I told her I was going to send her some card numbers for MoneyPak and to hang up and call me back after she got my text and loaded the money to her Walmart cards.

I forwarded the texts from Pierre to Jess and five minutes later, she called me and told me she loaded four cards each had $500 on them, and the balance on her card was now $2000. I told her to keep that money, and she said no. I told her she was going to take that money and that was it. She asked me how did I get that money, and I told her. She said no, she wasn't taking it. I did that for you, so you can get on your feet; I don't want the money. I told her she was taking the money and asked why she was giving me a hard time. She told me she would never go against me but would always be for me, and when I worded it that way, she said, "Okay fine, Lil' Riccy, even though that was dirty how you forced it on me to keep."

I laughed and said, "Like how you kinda forced the work on me."

I told her to go on out with her friends and to enjoy herself. She said, "Okay, daddy. I love you, and I will talk to you in the morning," I replied with ok in the morning, and we hung up. The police announced over the loud speaker five minutes to dayroom, so I put up my phone and prepared to head out.

JESS

*T*he night all in all was good. No fights broke out, and like I suspected, the chic was all too anxious to step in and help support Marcus' kids. She even paid for all of Marissa and Nikki's drinks. We left about an hour before closing, and on our way out, we saw Chuck heading towards the entrance.

"Look what we have here. Guess my wife being boss isn't working out, so you came here for your old job back, Marissa? And you, Jess, I never pictured you the type to take your clothes off, if so, I would have given you a promotion at the office," Chuck said

Wack!

Marissa smacked the dog shit out of him, and then I kicked him dead in his balls. I didn't know who the fuck he thought he was talking to, but I hoped next time, he thought twice.

"PeeWee, listen here, if my cousin and friend didn't already lay hands on you, I would walk over to that big, buff security guard and let him know you are harassing us and make sure I showed enough cleavage to where he would feel he had to beat your ass," Nikki added in. She never liked to feel left out.

"What seems to be going on over here?" Veronica, the girl kicking it with Marcus, said walking up to us. So, we filled her in on everything, and needless to say, Chuck would no longer be allowed there.   A bouncer had walked us to my car to make sure he didn't do anything, and we left. I just hoped Chuck didn't become a problem later on down the line.

I dropped Marissa off at home, told her to make sure she locked up, and put her alarm on. I waited until she was in the house, and I drove off. Nikki was crashing at my house tonight, so I drove on home. I just wanted to go home, text Lil' Riccy and let him know I was home and safe, and go to sleep. I had a long week, and I really just wanted to sleep in tomorrow. I knew that wasn't going to be the case. Me and sleep just didn't get along.

****

The next morning, I woke up, and Nikki was gone. She left a note saying she had to get to her mama's house to get the kids and would call me later. I looked at the time and couldn't believe it said it was 11:30 in the morning. I hadn't slept this late in a really long time. I climbed out the bed and went into the bathroom. I started the shower so the water could get hot, and I emptied my bladder. I grabbed my toothbrush and climbed in. I just let the hot, steamy water cascade down my body for a few minutes relaxing my sore muscles from all the shopping, and then being in heels all night. I then brushed my teeth, washed my hair and body, and then rewashed it. Once I was satisfied that I was clean enough, I turned the water off. I grabbed a towel to wrap my hair up in and then one for my body. I slipped my feet in my slippers and headed for my room. I picked up my phone. I wanted to make an appointment with a spa to get some waxing done. I was long overdue. I had a few missed calls and a text from Lil' Riccy. I must have really been out of it.

I had called the spa first because I knew I'd probably be on the phone with Lil' Riccy longer. Agreeing on me going in at four today, I had time to do a few loads of laundry and dust in the meantime. I put on a plain white tee and some panties and a pair of socks and texted my baby back. I missed him. We'd both been kind of busy lately and hadn't really chopped it up like we used to. I placed the phone down and began to sort the laundry. I had just finished putting in my first load when Lil' Riccy was calling me. I grabbed the phone and walked towards the living room. I answered and sat on the sofa and turned the TV on low.

"Hey, love," I said.

"Well hello to you. Long night? You are usually up and active by this time," he said.

"Not really, we left like an hour before last call. Chuck, the old boss, tried to start some drama. I hope it don't escalate, but otherwise, the night was all good. I guess I just needed the rest." "I see. So, what you doin' today?"

"I made an appointment at the spa to get a wax touch up. Until then, I'm just doing laundry and picking up the house. Not doing too much," I said.

"Oh okay, baby. Well, now that I know you are okay, I'm going to let you go do what you have to. I'll talk to you later." "Alright," I said, and I hung up.

This is what I mean. Lately, our conversations were quick and simple. I hoped everything was okay. Maybe me dropping that work on him wasn't a smart move to make without actually having a sit down and agreeing first. I got up and went to get me a water from the fridge. I turned the music on and began to clean the house. I cleaned places that didn't need to be touched. I just wanted to keep busy. Before I knew it, it was 2:30, so I hopped in a quick shower and tossed on some clothes and headed out to my appointment. After I was done, I was coming home and climbing in bed with a movie, and going to bed. I had work in the morning. What a life.

LIL' RICCY

I woke up early in the morning feeling good. I got out the bed and handled business so I could stretch and work out. After working out, I got my phone and called Jess. She answered on the first ring.

"Hey daddy," she said, sounding bright eyed and bushy tailed. "Good morning, ma. How did you sleep last night?" I asked her. "I slept good, and you, baby?" she asked me back.

"I slept good myself."

"I thought you was going to be mad at me for bringing that shit up there without asking you first," she said, kind of catching me off guard. I did feel something was off about her in our last conversation. I hoped she hadn't been trippin'.

"No, I wasn't mad, but I do wish you would have given me a heads up and asked me, but I know your intentions was good, and I know you was tryin' to help me, so how could I be mad at you for that, baby?"

"Sorry. I just been feeling like something has been off with us.

Knowing you ain't mad makes me feel better."

"Nothing you have done since we met has been wrong, girl. I swear you crazy," I said to lighten to conversation. "But hey, tell daddy what you got on right now."

"Like Adina Howard sang, I got my T-Shirt and My Panties On," Jess sang into the phone.

"Is that right? Let me hang up and call you on video. I need to see those pretty nipples and lower lips real quick before you get up for work."

"You don't have to ask twice," she said hanging up.

I called her on video chat, and we had a session of passion. Baby was a certified freak. No matter what I asked her to do, she complied. Knowing she didn't have hours, I rushed it in a sense that 30 minutes later, we were both satisfied, at least for now. She could go to work with a smile, and I was set for the day.

I told her that I needed her to go to Western Union and pick up the $2200 that Pierre had wired over, and I wanted her to put it up for me for when I came home. She told me she had already bought me a safe, and she would lock it up in it. I guess Jess was full of surprises. What else was in store for me? We hung up, and I did some writing. I called my mom and a few people I kicked it with in the free world from time to time.

They called breakfast. Now that I knew the homie Loon was safe and even protected, I decided I was going to stay back today. I made some oatmeal and just relaxed until it was time for me to go do yard work. I got up and dressed in my vest, and when I was leaving out my building, Pierre was calling me over. He told me he really needed more of that crystal and asked how long it would take me to get some. I guess me relaxing until I hit the streets wasn't going to happen. I told him I would call my people later and get back to him. I really needed to think about this. I'd see what she said. I didn't want to mess around and get more time added when I was so close to being free. I finally had a rider on my side, but that didn't mean I wanted baby girl to ride for years, even though her new saying had become *Her Heart Is On Lock.*

ABOUT THE AUTHORS

Soulja Choc was born and raised by his grandmother and mother in the streets of Watts, California. Gang banging, selling drugs, and messing with women was his perogative as a teenager, but at the age of 21, he became incarcerated, and is currently.

Though he has been through the struggle, his down time allowed him to find a legal hobby, thus giving life to his first novel, The Birth of the Gutta Squad.

Through personal experience and life trials, he has gone on to write several other books including Street Soulja 1 and 2, Ken 1 and 2: Finding the Missing Link, and several other short stories.

Author Chey was born and raised in Massachusetts. Growing up, she loved to read and expressing herself became a passion. Channeling her love for reading, she soon found herself on a new journey, telling her own stories. She loves to interact with new readers and often can be found in groups meeting new people.

Made in the USA
Columbia, SC
04 March 2018